JESS WAS THE BRAVE ONE

JEAN LITTLE
Illustrated by JANET WILSON

Puffin Books

For the real Claire and Jessica, who let me use their names in this book
J.L.

For my husband, Chris
J.W.

PUFFIN BOOKS
Published by the Penguin Group
Penguin Books Canada Ltd, 10 Alcorn Avenue, Toronto, Ontario, Canada M4V 3B2
Penguin Books Ltd, 27 Wrights Lane, London W8 5TZ, England
Penguin Books USA Inc., 375 Hudson Street, New York, New York 10014, U.S.A.
Penguin Books Australia Ltd, Ringwood, Victoria, Australia
Penguin Books (NZ) Ltd, 182-190 Wairau Road, Auckland 10, New Zealand

Penguin Books Ltd, Registered Offices: Harmondsworth, Middlesex, England

First published in Viking by Penguin Books Canada Limited, 1991

Published in Penguin Books, 1994

10 9 8 7 6 5 4 3 2 1

Text © Jean Little, 1991
Illustrations © Janet Wilson, 1991

Book Design: Bruce W. Bond

Publisher's note: This book is a work of fiction. Names, characters, places and incidents either are the product of the author's imagination or are used fictitiously, and any resemblance to actual persons living or dead, events, or locales is entirely coincidental.

Manufactured in Hong Kong

Canadian Cataloguing in Publication Data

Little, Jean, 1932-
    Jess was the brave one

ISBN 0-14-054309-0

I. Wilson, Janet, 1952-   . II. Title.

PS8523.I87J48 1992   jC813'.54   C91-093518-1
PZ7.L57Je 1992

British Library Cataloguing in Publication Data Available
American Library of Congress Cataloguing in Publication Data Available

Most nights, before Claire and Jess went to sleep, Mum or Dad read them a bedtime story.

But when Grandpa put them to bed, he did not read to them. He told them stories instead. He told them about men and women who had done brave deeds.

He told them about William Wilberforce and Harriet Tubman helping to free the slaves. He told them about the Duke of Wellington winning the battle of Waterloo.

Jess usually fell asleep before he finished. But Claire listened with shining eyes.

Claire longed to be brave. She pretended she was. She carried her dolls off battlefields and bandaged their wounds. She hid them from the slavecatchers. She tried to get Jess to play too.

"Let's pretend that Pink Ted has been kidnapped by bandits," she said to her little sister, "and we have to risk our lives going to his rescue."

Jess hugged her small, scruffy teddy bear close.

"Bandits wouldn't kidnap a teddy bear," she said. "I think it's stupid the way you keep pretending to be brave when you know you're not. I'm going in to watch TV."

Claire wanted to shout, "I am so brave!" But she knew she wasn't. Jess was the brave one.

Jess was brave when they went to the doctor's for shots. She held her arm out without fussing.

"That didn't hurt a bit," she said.

But Dad had to hold Claire's arm tightly or she would pull it away.

"This will feel like a mosquito bite," the doctor said.

"It doesn't feel like a mosquito," Claire sniffed. "It feels like a dagger."

"I'm afraid Claire suffers from an overactive imagination," Dad told the doctor.

Jess was also brave at bedtime. When Mum or Dad turned out the light and went downstairs, she shut her eyes and went to sleep.

Claire lay and stared into the darkness. She saw a black shape hiding behind the door. She thought she saw it move. She woke Jess.

"Oh, Claire, it's just our bathrobes," Jess said crossly. "Go to sleep."

Jess was brave when they climbed trees too. She always scrambled straight up to the top. Claire usually reached the second branch. Then she looked down.

"I'm going to fall," she bleated and shut her eyes. Jess had to climb back down and help her.

"You shouldn't think about falling," Jess said. "I never do. Just climb."

Jess was also brave when they met fierce dogs.

"Hi, boy," she would say, holding out her fingers for the dog to sniff.

"Jess, DON'T!" Claire would beg.

Next minute, the fierce dog would start wagging its tail and licking Jess's hand.

Then Claire would feel foolish even though she was positive that, someday, Jess was going to get bitten to the bone.

When something scary came on TV, Jess liked it. "Tell me when it's over," Claire moaned, putting a pillow over her head.

Sometimes, Jess thought it was funny to say it was over when it really wasn't. Then Claire would run into their bedroom and slam the door. She would not come out until Jess said she was sorry.

"Okay, okay. I'm sorry," Jess said. "But really, Claire, you are such a baby."

"I am not. I just have an overactive imagination," Claire said. She tried to sound proud, but she did not fool Jess.

Jess loved thunderstorms. She was not scared of witches or monsters or haunted houses.

"There are no such things as ghosts," Jess said.

There was no doubt about it.

Jess was the brave one.

Then, one Saturday morning, Claire heard Jess screaming. She ran outside to see what was wrong.

Jess was trying to grab something from some big kids. She was crying.

"Give him back," she was shouting. "Give Pink Ted back!"

Claire marched over and stood next to her little sister.

"You'd better give her back that bear," she said in a loud, clear voice, "or Wellington and Wilberforce will get you."

The tall boy looked down at her. He was holding Pink Ted up high where Jess could not reach. He was laughing.

"Who's going to get me?" he said.

Claire talked a tiny bit louder but she sounded very calm.

"Wellington and Wilberforce are our cousins," she said. "They are coming over in fifteen minutes. They are much bigger than you. MUCH bigger. Wilberforce is in the Navy. Wellington is a Police Chief."

"She's making it up," the shorter girl said. But she did not sound sure.

Jess had stopped crying. She was staring at her big sister.

"Wellington has a dragon tattooed on his chest," Claire said. "He hates bullies. And Wilberforce is a champion wrestler in his spare time. He gave Pink Ted to my sister. If anything happens to that bear, Wilberforce will be very, very mad!"

"I still think she's making it up," said the not-so-big boy, "but you'd better give back the kid's bear, just in case. Only babies like teddies anyway."

"Wilberforce is twenty-six," Claire said dreamily, "and he has a teddy bear collection. He keeps it with his judo stuff."

The big boy threw Pink Ted to Jess. "Take your dumb bear then," he said. "We have to get moving. Come on, you guys." They ran off down the street.

Jess clutched Pink Ted to her chest.

"Oh, Claire, you saved Pink Ted!" she said. "He really did get kidnapped by bandits. I was scared but you were as brave as a lion. How did you ever think up all that crazy stuff? Tell me more about those cousins of ours."

Claire thought for a moment.

"Wilberforce plays the mouth organ," she said, "and Wellington is double-jointed. He also has a very overactive imagination."